Lost!

Written by Christine Keighery

Illustrated by Julia Crouth

Kate was sad. She couldn't find her cat.

"Whiskers, Whiskers," she called. But the cat didn't come.

"Whiskers will come back," said her mother. "Put his food by the door."

3

When Kate came home from school, Whiskers was still missing. His food hadn't been eaten.

"Whiskers! Whiskers!" called Kate. But the cat didn't come.

"Maybe you should write a LOST notice," said her mother. "We could put it up in the store."

Kate went to the computer.
She thought about Whiskers.
Then she wrote a notice.

Kate printed the notice.
She showed it to her mother.

LOST!
My cat is lost.
He is the best cat in the world.
He purrs a lot.
He loves ice cream.
His name is Whiskers.

If you see him, please phone
Kate at 953-555-2699.

"That's good," said her mother.
"But if someone had never seen
Whiskers, how would they know
it was him?"

Kate thought about Whiskers some more. She wrote a new notice.

Kate printed the notice.
She showed it to her mother.

LOST!

My cat is lost.
He has short, black fur.
He has a pink tongue.
He has a long tail.
His name is Whiskers.
If you see him, please phone
Kate at 953-555-2699.

"That's better," said her mother.
"But all cats have pink tongues,
all cats have long tails.
What makes Whiskers different?"

Kate thought about Whiskers
some more, and she wrote
another notice.

Kate printed the notice.
She drew a picture of Whiskers.

LOST!

My cat is lost.

He has short, black fur.

He has a white patch over his left eye.

He has a red collar with a little bell.

His name is Whiskers.

If you see him,
please phone Kate
at 953-555-2699.

Kate showed the notice
to her mother.

"That's great, Kate!"
her mother said.

They took the notice to the store
and put it on the notice board.
"I hope you find your cat,"
said the man at the store.

Kate waited and waited for
someone to phone her.
But nobody did.

"Let's put copies of the notice
in some other stores," said Kate's
mother. "This time, we'll put a
photo of Whiskers on the notice."

Kate found a photo of Whiskers.
They scanned the photo into
the computer.

Then Kate and her mother printed
some copies. They put them up
in different stores.

That night, the phone rang.
"Is this Kate?" asked a lady.
"I think I might have your cat."

"Does he have short, black fur?" asked Kate.

"Yes," said the lady.

"Does he have a white patch over his left eye?" asked Kate.

"Yes," said the lady.

"Does he have a red collar with a bell?" asked Kate.

"Yes, yes, yes," laughed the lady. "And he purrs a lot, too. Listen!"

The lady told Kate where she lived.

Kate and her mother went
to get Whiskers.

"Is that him?" asked the lady.
"He seems to like ice cream."

"That's him," said Kate's mother.
"He loves ice cream."

"Whiskers! Whiskers!" called Kate.

Whiskers looked up. He ran
to Kate. Kate picked him up.
Whiskers rubbed his face against
Kate's chin. He purred and purred.

"I found Whiskers sleeping in
my car," said the lady.
"I knew someone would be
looking for him. Luckily, I saw
your notice."

Kate laughed and laughed.
"I forgot to say in my notice that
Whiskers loves cars!" she said.